4/16 S4x 10/15

Aunt Eater's Mystery Christmas

Story and pictures by

Doug Cushman

HarperCollins*Publishers*

TO
Linda
and
Larry

HarperCollins®, 📖®, and I Can Read Book®
are trademarks of HarperCollins Publishers Inc.

AUNT EATER'S MYSTERY CHRISTMAS
Copyright © 1995 by Doug Cushman
Printed in the U.S.A. All rights reserved.

Library of Congress Cataloging-in-Publication Data
Cushman, Doug.
    Aunt Eater's mystery Christmas / story and pictures by Doug
Cushman.
        p.   cm. — (An I can read book)
    Summary: Aunt Eater must interrupt her holiday preparations to
solve some Christmas Eve mysteries.
    ISBN 0-06-023579-9. — ISBN 0-06-023580-2 (lib. bdg.)
    [1. Anteaters—Fiction.   2. Christmas—Fiction.   3. Mystery and
detective stories.]   I. Title.   II. Series.
PZ7.C959Aun   1995   94-30714
[E]—dc20   CIP
                                                                        AC

3   4   5   6   7   8   9   10
❖

CONTENTS

Aunt Eater Orders Some Tea

Bump!

"Excuse me," said Aunt Eater.

Bump! Bump!

"Pardon me. Excuse me."

It was Christmas Eve.

Aunt Eater the anteater

was shopping downtown.

5

"It is so crowded," she said.

"I'm glad that I'm done

with my Christmas shopping.

Now I must go home

and clean the house

before my sister, Eliza, arrives."

Aunt Eater passed a bookstore.

A sign in the window said:

Read
Edna Herring's
New Mystery!

"I love mysteries," said Aunt Eater,
"and she is my favorite author.
I will buy the book
as a present to myself."
She went inside.

"I'm sorry," said the clerk.

"We sold out an hour ago."

"Oh dear," said Aunt Eater.

"Maybe some tea and cookies

will cheer me up."

She sat down in Lacey's Tea Shop.

Suddenly she saw

a scrap of paper on the floor.

It said:

Rob-Frampton's Jewelry
Store
Pearl and Ruby-rings
12 o'clock

"Goodness!" she cried.

"Someone is going to rob

the jewelry store!

I must find a police officer."

Aunt Eater ran out of the tea shop.

She turned the corner and

CRASH!

She ran into Officer Miles.

"What's the hurry?" he asked.

Aunt Eater showed him the note.

"We must get to the jewelry store!"

said Officer Miles.

"It is almost twelve o'clock!"

They ran inside the store.

"I'm here for the rings,"

said a dark figure to the clerk.

"Stop!" cried Aunt Eater.

Just then a lady walked in.

"Hello, Rob," she said.

"I'm sorry if I'm late.

I lost my shopping list

and could not remember

when we were going to meet."

15

"What's going on here?"

asked Officer Miles.

"My son Rob and I came

to pick up the presents

for my grandchildren,"

said the lady.

"This year I am giving them

rings to match their names—

Ruby and Pearl."

"What a nice surprise for them,"

said Aunt Eater.

"And what a surprise for us,"

said Officer Miles.

"Yes," said Aunt Eater.

"Christmas can be full of surprises.

You never know what might happen.

18

Now I must hurry home

and get ready for Eliza."

Now I must hurry home
and get ready for Eliza."

 Aunt Eater Takes Out the Garbage

Aunt Eater walked to the bus stop.

On the way

she saw another bookstore.

"Maybe *this* bookstore

has Edna Herring's new book,"

she said.

But a sign in the window said:

SOLD OUT.

"I will *never* get that book,"

said Aunt Eater,

and she got on the bus.

23

When Aunt Eater got home,

she cleaned the house

for Eliza's visit.

She dusted every room

and took the garbage outside.

Suddenly she saw

a mysterious man with a white beard

go behind Mr. Fragg's house.

"That did not look like
Mr. Fragg," said Aunt Eater.
"That man could be a thief!
I will see what he is doing."
Aunt Eater sneaked around
to the back of the house.

The mysterious man

was climbing in the window.

"Goodness!" she cried.

"You *are* a thief!"

"Please help me!"

the man said.

"I am stuck!"

"I will not help a thief!"

cried Aunt Eater.

"But I am your neighbor,"

said the man.

"You are not Mr. Fragg,"

said Aunt Eater.

"Yes I am!" said the man.

He took off his beard.

"Mr. Fragg!" said Aunt Eater.

She helped him out of the window.

"Thank you," said Mr. Fragg.

"That is much better."

"Why were you climbing

in your own window?"

asked Aunt Eater.

"I forgot my house keys,"

said Mr. Fragg.

"I knew this window was unlocked.

I wanted to climb through,

but I am too fat."

"Why do you have that beard?"

asked Aunt Eater,

"and how did you get so fat?"

"This is my costume,"

said Mr. Fragg.

"I am pretending to be Santa Claus

at a Christmas party."

"You will make a jolly Santa,"

said Aunt Eater,

"and there is no mystery about that!"

"Ho, ho, ho!" laughed Mr. Fragg.

Aunt Eater  Follows Some Tracks

When Aunt Eater went home,

she said, "Oh dear!

I forgot to give Mrs. Plum

and her twins

a plate of Christmas cookies.

I will do it now before Eliza comes."

She knocked on Mrs. Plum's door.

"I am so glad to see you!"

said Mrs. Plum.

"I have a real mystery for you.

Come inside!"

"I was making some soup,"

said Mrs. Plum.

"I left the kitchen

for a few minutes.

When I returned,

my new hat and coat were gone!"

"How strange," said Aunt Eater.

"It gets even stranger,"

said Mrs. Plum.

"I am also missing

the carrot for my soup!"

"Let's look for some clues,"

said Aunt Eater.

They looked around the kitchen.

Aunt Eater spotted

some puddles of water.

"These look like footprints,"

she said,

"and they seem to go outside."

They followed the footprints
to the fence.
"The thief went this way,"
said Aunt Eater. "Follow me."
They crawled through a hole.

The footprints went up a hill

and down.

They went around a large rock
and into a big field.

"Look!" said Mrs. Plum.

"That person has my hat and coat!
She must be the thief!"

Suddenly Aunt Eater began to laugh.

"I think this mystery is solved,"

she said.

"Oh dear!" said Mrs. Plum.

"It is a snowman!

And there are the twins.

They must have taken

my hat and coat

and used the carrot for the nose!"

"One thing is for sure,"

said Aunt Eater.

"It is the best dressed

snowman in town."

45

Aunt Eater  Finds a Present

That night the doorbell rang.

"Eliza!" cried Aunt Eater.

"It is so good to see you."

"I brought Sally," said Eliza.

"She could not stay home alone

for Christmas."

"I am happy to see her too,"

said Aunt Eater.

47

Aunt Eater and Eliza

trimmed the tree.

Then they ate

a big Christmas Eve dinner

and sang carols.

Then it was time for bed.

Aunt Eater put out

a blanket and pillow for Sally.

"Good night, Sally," she said.

Aunt Eater and Eliza went upstairs.

"Sweet dreams," said Eliza.

"Good night," said Aunt Eater,

and she crawled into bed.

Suddenly she heard

THUMP!

"What was that?" she said.

She tiptoed downstairs

and switched on the light.

"Oh, it is only you, Sally,"

said Aunt Eater.

"Come out of the garbage can."

Aunt Eater got back into bed.

She was almost asleep

when suddenly she heard

BUMP!

"Now what was that?" she asked.

She went downstairs.

"I see you found a mousehole,"
said Aunt Eater.

"Try to be a little more quiet."

Aunt Eater went back to bed.

But a few minutes later she heard

Jingle! Jingle!

then THUMP!

Aunt Eater sighed.

"What is that cat up to now?"

she said.

She went downstairs,

but Sally was sound asleep.

"What made that noise?"

asked Aunt Eater.

"Could it be a thief?"

Suddenly she saw a huge shadow.

"Somebody is in the house!"

she said.

She hid behind the door.

Then the shadow was gone.

Aunt Eater looked out

and saw something

under the Christmas tree.

"It's a present," said Aunt Eater,

"and it's for me.

I did not see it before.

I wonder who it is from?"

She opened the present.

"Oh my!" she cried.

"It's Edna Herring's new book!

How did it get here?

Who gave it to me?

This *is* a mystery.

I will look for some clues."

She saw some footprints

around the tree.

They stopped at the fireplace.

Just then Aunt Eater heard

Jingle! Jingle!

She looked outside and saw

a dark shape in the sky.

"Christmas is filled with
some wonderful mysteries,"
said Aunt Eater, and sat down
to read her new book.

"*Meow*," said Sally.

"Merry Christmas to you too,"
said Aunt Eater.